GROWING THINGS

Angela Wilkes
Illustrated by John Shackell

CONTENTS

With thanks to Roger Priddy

How plants grow

IT IS QUITE EASY TO GROW THINGS. BUT FIRST YOU HAVE TO UNDERSTAND WHAT MAKES PLANTS GROW AND GIVE THEM WHAT THEY NEED

Watching things grow

Roll about six sheets of paper towels into a tube and slide it into a big glass jar. Push different kinds of beans down between the jar and the paper. Wet the paper, then pour some water into the jar to keep the paper wet.

Put the jar in a warm place and look at it every day. The water will make the beans swell and split, then they will sprout. Watch what happens to the roots and shoots.

A PLANT CANNOT LIVE ON WATER ALONE. IF YOU WANT YOUR BEAN PLANTS TO GROW BIG, PUT THEM IN POTS WHEN THEY ARE ABOUT 6 in TALL. (See page 18)

Things plants need

Plants need light for them to grow and make green leaves.

ALL PLANTS NEED WATER, BUT TOO MUCH WATER IS AS BAD FOR THEM AS TOO LITTLE. THEY LIKE RAINWATER BETTER THAN TAP WATER

Pots have holes in the bottom so water can drain out. If the soil gets soggy the roots of the plant will rot and die.

Gravel or bits of broken pot over the holes in the pots stop them from getting blocked, so that water can drain out of them easily.

A saucer under the pot catches the water.

YOU CAN BUY LIQUID PLANT FOOD. YOU ADD IT TO WATER AND POUR IT ON THE SOIL TO REPLACE THE FOOD THE PLANT HAS USED UP

Plants get their food and water from the soil. Their roots grow best in light, crumbly soil with a little peat and sand.

Potting soil for house plants is light soil with rich plant food in it.

REMEMBER THAT PLANTS ARE LIVING THINGS. LOOK AFTER THEM CAREFULLY AND THEY WILL GROW STRONG AND HEALTHY

3

Sowing seeds

Potting soil

seeds

Watering can

seed tray

sunflowers   zinnia   nasturtiums

An annual grows from seed, flowers and dies in one year.

foxgloves   pansies   sweet william

A biennial lives for two years. You plant it one year and it usually flowers the second year.

geraniums   fuchsia

irises   peonies

A perennial lives and flowers for many years. It usually dies down in the winter, but grows again the next spring.

IF YOU PLANT SEEDS INDOORS IN SPRING THE SEEDLINGS WILL BE BIG ENOUGH TO PLANT OUTSIDE WHEN THE WEATHER IS WARM ENOUGH

Fill a seed tray with potting soil. Sprinkle the seeds over it, then cover them lightly with more soil.

Water the seeds gently, using a watering can with a fine spray.

Tie a plastic bag over the tray and put it in a warm, dark place. The bag helps keep the soil damp.

As soon as shoots appear, take the box out of the bag and put it in a warm, light place.

When the plants have six leaves, replant them 2in. apart in new trays, so they have more room to grow.

As soon as the weather is warm enough, move the trays outside, so the plants get used to being outdoors.

When they have grown too big for the trays, dig them up very carefully, keeping the soil around their roots.

Dig small holes in the garden and carefully plant the seedlings in them. Press the soil down around them, then water them.

Sunflowers

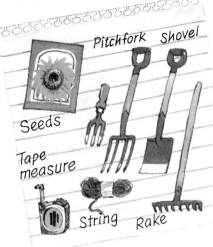

Seeds
Pitchfork
Shovel
Tape measure
String
Rake

Giant sunflowers grow very fast. You can plant the seeds outside.

Plant the seeds in the spring. Choose a sunny place with good soil, near a fence or a wall if possible.

Pull up all the weeds, then dig and rake the ground, so the soil is level and does not have any lumps in it.

Water the ground every day and shoots will appear in 10-14 days. The plants will grow very fast if you remember to water them. You could have a race with a friend to see whose sunflower grows the fastest (or tallest).

Push the seeds into the ground about ½in. deep and 24in. apart, so they have room to grow.

TIE THE SUNFLOWER TO A STICK AS IT GROWS, TO STOP IT FROM FLOPPING OVER

Sunflowers grow 9-13 feet tall. Measure them every week. They flower from July to September.

The flowers are the size of dinner plates and turn around to face the sun. Bees love them.

When the flowers die, cut off one of the heads and rub the seeds out onto some newspaper with a fork.

Put the seeds in an envelope. Seal it and label it, then keep it in a dry place and plant the seeds next year.

Growing trees

Pots and saucers

Potting soil

Pebbles

Pitchfork

Plastic bags

Plant a tree. In ten years it will be a home for many birds and insects, and it may live to be hundreds of years old.

1 Acorns

2 Ash seeds

3 Holly berries

4 Beech nuts

5 Pine cone

6 Chestnut

You can grow trees from acorns, chestnuts and any other tree seeds you find in autumn. Keep a note of what you find, so you know which seedling is what later on. You can also collect fruit seeds to plant.

Plastic bag

Saucer

Plant each seed in a small pot. Water it, then tie a plastic bag over the pot. This keeps the soil damp.

Put the pots on a windowsill or in a sunny place. Most seeds take two months or longer to sprout, so you must be patient. Take the plastic bags off as soon as the seedlings appear and water the baby trees every week.

Plant the trees outside in autumn. Do not put them too near houses as they will grow long roots. Dig holes a bit bigger than the pots.

Plant each tree in a hole and put a strong cane in next to it. Fill in the soil and press it down, tie the tree to the cane, then water it.

Matching seeds and leaves

A

B

C

D

E

F

I PLANTED THIS TREE WHEN I WAS YOUR AGE

You can find out what a tree is by looking at its leaves. Can you match these leaves with the seeds on the opposite page? The answers are at the side of the page.

Keep a tree sketchbook and draw new trees you see. Or keep a diary about a tree and write down when the leaves and seeds appear.

Answer: 1D, 2C, 3E, 4A, 5F, 6B.

9

Planting bulbs

BULBS ARE EASY TO GROW INDOORS. PLANT THEM IN THE AUTUMN AND THEY WILL FLOWER IN THE WINTER AND SPRING

CROCUS

DAFFODIL

BLUEBELL

SNOWDROP

TULIP

Most of the first spring flowers grow from bulbs, which are a kind of underground food store. These plants rest for part of the year then use the food in the bulbs to grow in spring. When the leaves die they send food back to the bulb.

If you cut a bulb in half you can see the baby plant inside, ready to grow.

Half fill your pots with potting soil. Put the bulbs on top, pointed end up and close together, then fill the pots with more soil. Small bulbs must be covered. Big ones can poke out of the soil. Water them.

PUT THE POTS IN A COOL, DARK PLACE FOR 8-10 WEEKS AND THE BULBS WILL START TO GROW. THEY WILL ONLY GROW WHEN IT IS COOL. CHECK THE SOIL NOW AND THEN TO SEE IT IS DAMP

When the buds are about 2in. high, put the pots in a light but cool place. Water the plants regularly.

KEEP THE WATER LEVEL UP

Growing a hyacinth in water

Fill a bulb jar with water to just below the bulb. Put it in a dark place until the roots are 4in. long. A few bits of charcoal in the water help to keep it clean.

When they are taller, move them to a warmer place. Push in sticks to support droopy plants. When the flowers die, cut off the heads but leave the leaves. Plant the bulbs outside if you can as they won't flower indoors again.

Window boxes

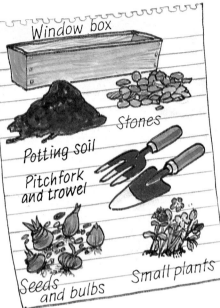

Window box
Stones
Potting soil
Pitchfork and trowel
Seeds and bulbs
Small plants

YOU CAN PUT POTS ON THE WINDOW LEDGE INSTEAD, AS LONG AS THEY ARE SECURE AND CAN'T FALL OFF

You need a strong, deep window ledge for a window box. A box full of soil is heavy and must be safe. Ask an adult to set yours up for you. It is best if the box tilts back a little, so wedge pieces of wood under the front edge.

Filling the box

POTTING SOIL IS BETTER THAN GARDEN SOIL AS IT CONTAINS ALL THE FOOD YOUR PLANTS NEED TO GROW STRONG AND HEALTHY

Planting

Dig a small hole for each plant. Put it in carefully so the roots have enough room, then press down the soil.

Put a layer of gravel or broken pots in the bottom of your box. This stops the soil from getting soggy. Fill the rest of the box with potting soil and rake it to make it level.

12

You can grow bulbs, seeds and plants in your window box. Find out when different plants flower, then plan what to plant. Do you know what the flowers in these window boxes are?

Spring

ALWAYS PLANT TALL FLOWERS AT THE BACK OF THE BOX AND SMALL ONES AT THE FRONT

Bulbs flower in spring (see page 10). When they have finished flowering, dig them up, rake the soil and plant seeds for summer flowers.

Summer

You can grow flowers from seed for the summer or put in small plants. The soil in window boxes dries out quickly, so remember to water it often.

Autumn

CUT OFF THE DEAD FLOWER HEADS TO MAKE YOUR PLANTS KEEP FLOWERING

These flowers bloom until the first frosts. Put geraniums in pots and bring them indoors for the winter. Plant spring bulbs early in autumn.

Winter

Winter is the resting time for plants. Cut off dead leaves, pull up weeds and rake over the soil. Then wait for the first spring shoots to appear.

Spring: tulips, forget-me-nots, grape hyacinths.
Summer: marigolds, morning glory, daisies

Autumn: geraniums, lobelia
Winter: snowdrops

13

Growing herbs

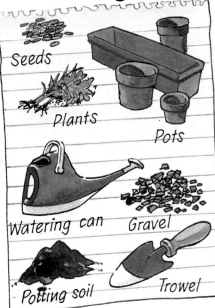

Seeds

Plants

Pots

Watering can

Gravel

Potting soil

Trowel

Cooking

Perfumes

Medicine

People have grown herbs for thousands of years. They have used them to flavor food and to make perfumes and medicines. In the past many people even thought that herbs had magic powers and could keep witches away.

SNIFF SNIFF

An herb's scent comes from oils in its leaves. You smell them if you crush a leaf. Cooks chop herbs to bring out the flavor.

You can buy herbs as plants or grow them from seed (see page 4). You can grow them in the garden, in window boxes or in flowerpots on a sunny windowsill. Herbs need well-drained soil, so if you grow them in pots, remember to put some gravel or broken pot in the bottom.

14

Parsley

This only lives for one year. It is best to buy plants. It likes some shade and a lot of water.

Thyme

Likes shade. Keep soil damp. Pick leaves as you need them.

YOU CAN DRY THYME BY TYING BUNCHES OF IT UPSIDE DOWN IN AN AIRY PLACE FOR TWO WEEKS. WHEN IT IS DRY, RUB THE LEAVES OFF THE STEMS AND PUT THEM IN AN AIRTIGHT JAR

Mint

Small shrub. Likes sun. Bees like the flowers.

Rosemary

Evergreen shrub. Grows up to 6½ feet tall. Likes a sunny, sheltered place.

PICK HERBS AS YOU NEED THEM. ALWAYS CUT A GROWING SHOOT AS THIS MAKES THE PLANT GROW STRONG AND BUSHY

Tarragon

Needs a sunny, sheltered place. Grows up to three feet tall.

DO NOT LET YOUR HERBS FLOWER IF YOU ARE GOING TO USE THEM FOR COOKING. PICK OFF FLOWER BUDS AND THE LEAVES WILL GROW MORE BUSHY

Chives

Grow in clumps. Pink flowers. Need a lot of water. Have an oniony taste.

Tomatoes

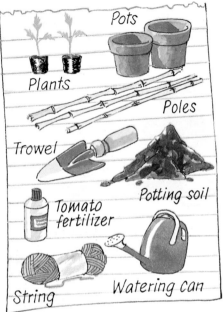

Plants
Pots
Poles
Trowel
Tomato fertilizer
Potting soil
String
Watering can

Tall one-stemmed plant
Small bush plant
Ordinary
Beefsteak
Cherry
Yellow
Plum

Home-grown tomatoes taste much better than the ones you buy in shops. You can grow them from seed (see page 4) or buy small plants, and you can grow them indoors or outdoors, as long as they have a sunny, sheltered spot.

Planting

Fill a big pot, about 10in. across, with potting soil. Put a pole in it and dig a small hole.

Tip the plant out of its pot, keeping all the soil around its roots, and plant it in the big pot.

Fill in more soil around it and press it down firmly. Then give the soil a good watering.

The growing plant

Put your plant in a warm, sunny place. Water it often to keep the soil damp. Tie the plant loosely to to the pole as it grows taller. When it flowers, shake it gently once a day. This helps to scatter the pollen.

Pinch off side shoots that grow where the leaf stalks join the stem. This makes the plant grow stronger.

Pick the tomatoes when they are ripe and red, with the stalk still on the tomato.

When there are four bunches of tomatoes on the plant, pinch off the top shoot to stop it growing.

Growing beans

WHEN THE BEANS REACH THE TOP OF THE POLES, PINCH OFF THE TOP GROWING SHOOTS

You don't need a garden to grow vegetables. Here are some you can grow in pots on a balcony or patio.

Fill a bucket-sized pot with potting soil. Stick three poles in it and tie them together at the top to make a climbing frame.

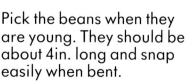

Plant a seed next to each stick and water them. Shoots will appear in 2-3 weeks. As the stems grow, twist them around the poles.

Water the soil often to keep it damp. When flowers appear, spray them with water. This helps the pods to grow.

Pick the beans when they are young. They should be about 4in. long and snap easily when bent.

Potatoes

THE SOIL MUST STAY DAMP, SO DON'T FORGET TO WATER IT

Find a sprouting potato and put it on a warm windowsill until the shoots are 1in. long. Leave two shoots and rub the rest off.

Put stones in the bottom of a 10in. pot and half fill it with potting compost. Plant the potato with the shoots at the top and water it. In about a month green shoots will appear. Add enough compost to cover them. Keep doing this as the shoots grow until the bucket is full.

After a while the plant will flower. Stop watering it when the flowers die, as the baby potatoes will rot if the soil is too wet.

Wait until the whole plant dies, then tip the pot out onto newspaper and see how many potatoes you have grown.

Houseplants

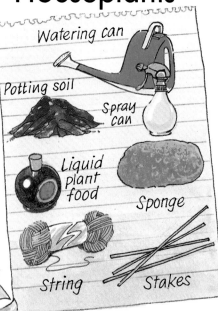

Watering can

Potting soil

Spray can

Liquid plant food

Sponge

String

Stakes

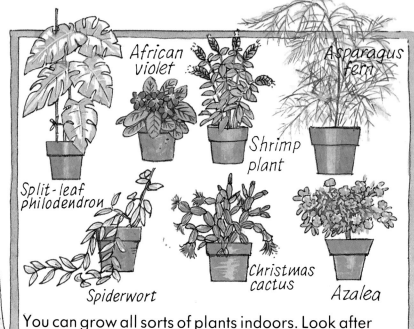

Split-leaf philodendron

African violet

Shrimp plant

Asparagus fern

Spiderwort

Christmas cactus

Azalea

You can grow all sorts of plants indoors. Look after them carefully and watch out for insect pests.

Buying a plant

NEVER OVERWATER A PLANT AS THIS CAN KILL IT

When you buy a plant, read its label or look in a book to see what kind of light and warmth it needs before you decide where to put it. Some plants like light and others shade. None of them like to be in a drafty place.

Water a plant when its soil is dry and more often in hot weather. It is often best to put water in the saucer, not on the plant.

Looking after your plants

Spray plants with water from time to time to clean them. Wipe dusty leaves with a damp cloth and cut off dead leaves and flower heads.

A tall plant needs support to keep it from flopping over. Put a stake in the soil and tie the stems to it loosely as the plant grows.

Plants grow faster in the spring and summer. You can make them grow bushier by picking off the growing tips of the shoots.

You can have an indoor garden in any light room in the house.

I TALK TO MY PLANTS WHEN I'M IN THE BATHTUB

When a plant's roots are too big for its pot, repot it in a larger pot, with new soil. Water it and put it in a shady place for a week.

21

Making baby plants

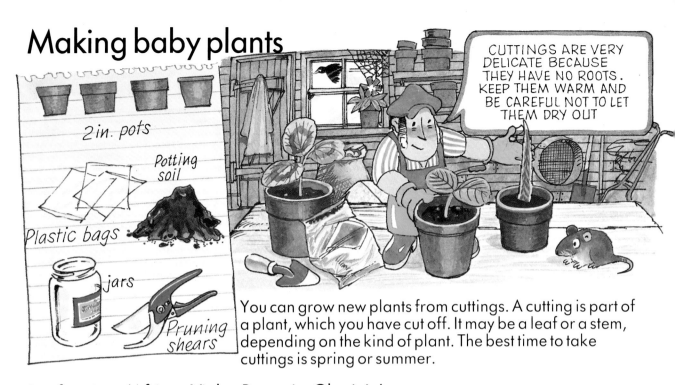

2 in. pots

Potting soil

Plastic bags

jars

Pruning shears

CUTTINGS ARE VERY DELICATE BECAUSE THEY HAVE NO ROOTS. KEEP THEM WARM AND BE CAREFUL NOT TO LET THEM DRY OUT

You can grow new plants from cuttings. A cutting is part of a plant, which you have cut off. It may be a leaf or a stem, depending on the kind of plant. The best time to take cuttings is spring or summer.

Leaf cuttings (African Violet, Begonia, Gloxinia)

Cut a healthy leaf and its stem off a plant. Plant the stem in a pot of cutting soil. Water it, cover it with a jar and put it in a warm, light place.

Baby plants will appear at the bottom of the leaf stem in about six weeks. When they look strong enough you can separate them and plant each one in its own pot.

Stem cuttings (Geraniums, Spiderwort)

Cut off a strong shoot about 4in. long, just below a leaf. Trim off the bottom leaves. Fill a small pot with cuttings compost.

Gently plant the cutting up to its leaves. Water it, cover it with a plastic bag and put it in a warm place out of the sun.

After a week or two take the bag off and pull the cutting gently. If it feels firm, it has rooted and you can leave the bag off.

A spider plant grows baby plants with roots at the end of runners. When the roots are about 1in. long, cut the baby plants off the runners and plant them in small pots of compost, making sure their roots are covered.

Plant presents

Look after your baby plants and you can give your friends presents you have grown yourself.

Garden calendar

This calendar is a guide to when to plant the things in this book. The times shown go from the earliest date you can plant something to the latest date. They can change a bit from one year to another, depending on how cold the weather is.

Name	Spring	Summer	Autumn
Flowers	▦ ▦ ⋰ ⬗	⬗ ✿ ✿	✿
Trees			⬗ ⬗
Tomatoes	▦ ⋰ ⬗	⬗ ↯ ↯	↯
Bulbs	✿ ✿ ✿		⬗ ⬗
Herbs	▦ ⬗	↯ ↯ ↯ ↯	↯
Sun-Flowers	⋰ ⬗ ⬗	✿ ✿	✿
Beans	⋰ ⬗	⬗ ↯ ↯ ↯	↯
Potatoes	⬗ ⬗ ↯	↯ ↯	

Key: ▦ seeds indoors   ⋰ seeds outdoors   ⬗ plant
⬗ pick   ✿ flowers

READ THE BACKS OF SEED PACKETS TO FIND OUT EXACTLY WHEN TO PLANT DIFFERENT KINDS OF SEEDS

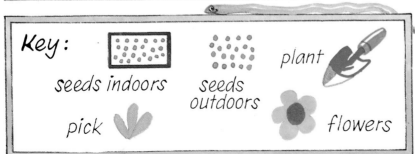